# R★WHEAD

# Another Beautiful Day As A Corpse And Other Stories

By

Noel K Hannan

First published in 2023

by Rawhead

an imprint of Ankh Digital

Book design by Noel K Hannan

Cover illustration by Rik Rawling

Interior illustrations by Andrw Sawyers, Mister Hughes, Andrew Richmond, Rik Rawling, Laurence Alison, Jaroslaw Ejsymont and Marina Tsareva

All rights reserved

© Noel K Hannan, 2023

Printed by Amazon

Lyrics to As Time Goes By by Herman Hupfeld used with respect, but without permission. Sorry.

Any resemblance to living persons in this work of fiction is entirely satirical.

The right of Noel K Hannan to be identified as author of this work has been asserted in accordance with Section 77 of the Copyright, Designs and Patents Act 1988

*To PDawg,
of course,
with love once again*

*Never, ever stop……*

# Foreword

When I wrote Things to Do in Derby When You're Dead in 2021, in a world still just about shaking off the COVID-19 pandemic like a wet dog climbing from the river, I had no idea it would be one of the most successful pieces of work I have ever created. Having started my professional creative career with zombies (Night of the Living Dead, 1993), a return to the subject matter almost 30 years later did not immediately indicate to me that I was back on track. But the reaction (see the review quotes on the back cover) and subsequent sales of the book took me completely by surprise. Modest by any standards, but stratospheric in comparison to anything I had put forward in my (so far) lacklustre creative career.

So.....a bit more to come, obviously. Having been pressed into getting the first book to the printers by my muse, partner, best friend and creative sounding board, Paula White, what you are about to read is the end result of many formal creative hot-housing forums with her aka breakfast and waking up with "You will not believe what I dreamt last night." As a personal purveyor of technicolour Michael Bay/Ridley Scott kinetic dreams, I can only marvel at what goes on in Paula's head during the silent hours. And I fastidiously write it all down.

So....what to expect in this new book? Well, we start with an ill-fated (spoiler, but you knew that anyway) gunboat diplomacy expedition to Haiti. It doesn't end well - does it ever? I will not spoil the heraldic interlude.......We then move on to meet our new hero Terry Mickle on the Mean Streets of Birmingham, then our first fully sentient Chewman, and finally get a scientific (sort of) take on the whole shitshow.

And it was a lot of fun to write.

So...let's get on with it.

Will you enjoy it as much as the first outing?

There is, as ever, only one way to find out.......


Noel K Hannan
Hereford and Birmingham
Spring 2023

# RECAP!

*(for full effect, this section needs to be read in the voice of General Stanley McChrystal).*

Britain. The very near and not totally unbelievable future.

COVID-19 has been and gone and, in its wake, comes the **VIRAX**, a pandemic on steroids which turns its victims into **INSTATIABLE FLESH EATING ZOMBIES!!!!!**

The planet is ravaged by this plague and the UK government stands alone in its world-beating resolve to combat......no, we're just kidding, it is of course as equally shit as everyone else, and probably worst than most.

COBRA convenes, makes pronouncements, sets policy, all useless. The Chewmans roll over the country, the continent, the world.

Is there any hope? Maybe....the remnants of authority try to re-establish law and order, to no avail. The detritus of the UK government is driven north, to the sparsely populated regions of Northern England and Scotland, eventually setting up base in Balmoral Castle. This move will not end well......

*(Admit it, you Googled Stan and then imitated, his voice, didn't you? I know I did)*

Now, read on............

# VOODOO CHILD

**Illustration by Andrw Sawyers**

*(the events of this story take place during the story Ministry of Z, from the original collection Things To Do In Derby When You're Dead)*

I am not allowed to say how many sailors, marines and airmen lost their lives in Haiti, but I counted them out.
And few of them came back.

The government of the day will rue its decision to send the punitive expedition to Haiti in search of the elusive origin of Patient Zero. It was launched at a point where public opinion was still a thing to be courted, considered and measured, and when there was still a significant public to generate such an opinion. These things are artefacts from the past now. Much like *The Sentinel* newspaper I was writing this eye-witness account for.

Of course, the only reason I was allowed on to the assault carrier HMS REPUDIATE as an embedded journalist was to report favourably on this incredibly foolhardy, wasteful and jingoistic example of gunboat diplomacy, which you would think had been resigned to history and the Americans, especially when you recall the eventual critical role the Royal Navy played in what passed for the subsequent post-pandemic recovery. A small task force had been assembled comprising of HMS REPUDIATE, with its Merlin helicopters and a half-Commando of Royal Marines (specifically 22.5 Commando if I recall correctly[1]), the hunter-killer submarine HMS ALBATROSS (presumably to protect the mission against zombie sharks and whales!.....more of which later.....), and the PFI[2] frigates HMS SERCO and HMS CAPITA, who would provide MVP-FP[3] for the mission along with communications services currently outsourced to India. And sail this little ad hoc force did, in silence and in the dead of night from Fountain Lake Jetty, Portsmouth, in order to take advantage of affordable follow-the-sun call centre support, in case of unforeseen IT issues.

Average transit time across the Atlantic Portsmouth-Haiti (admittedly, not a particularly popular route) is around 14 days. This period allowed me the opportunity to move around the ship and talk to

---

[1] *A daft in joke. A Commando (or Cdo), in this sense of the word, is a military body of Royal Marines equivalent to an Army battalion, comprising anything between 300 to 1000 personnel. There are 3 infantry-roled Cdos in 3 Commando Brigade – 40, 42 and 45 – plus five supporting Cdos. So if half of 45 Cdo deployed to Haiti, then you could refer to it as 22.5 Commando. If you wanted to.*
[2] *Private Finance Initiative*
[3] *Minimum Viable product - Force Protection*

the noticeably young crew members, sometimes formally (courtesy of the young female Lieutenant I referred to as my 'Political Commissar'[4]) and more often than not, informally over the galley[5] hotplate and smattering of illegal bars which littered the vessel (including one I had set up myself in my cabin for that express purpose). Unsurprisingly, the informal encounters supplied much more telling information than the formal ones. Here is a scattering of anecdotes:

Surname: Smith
First Name: Kylie
Rank and Role: Rating, Weapons Technician
Age: 19
Marital Status: single

Kylie is a diminutive and pleasant young lady from Newcastle who joined the Royal Navy at age 18 after a short abortive first career as a social media influencer. That is as hard a career choice as manning the Goalkeeper, a Close In Weapons Systems (CIWS[6]) on a modern warship, and I make no bones about fist-bumping Kylie of that fact. Kylie, in return, provides me with the following nuggets of intelligence and, on occasion, wisdom:

"You know we're not expected to survive, right? That's why there's so many single people on this voyage. It's like fuckin' Tinder 18-30! I've had 27 expressions of interest so far!"
How does that make you feel?
"Well.........wanted........? I guess. But it's also a bit weird, right? I mean, generally we are not encouraged to, what's the word, fraternise? But on this trip, it's like the opposite, everyone is at it like rabbits!"
And why do you think that is?

---

[4] A sarcastic reference to the practice of Soviet Forces in WW2 having officers attached to frontline units to ensure Communist principles and direction were upheld. In reality, this hapless young Lieutenant had done an online training session in Media Skills

[5] A kitchen and dining area on a ship

[6] A fast-firing automated cannon, usually of a medium calibre 20mm-40mm, designed to shoot down fast attacking jets or antiship missiles

"Well, like I said, we are not expected to survive......so who <u>literally</u> gives a fuck?"

Surname: Jones
First Name: David (Davy)
Rank and Role: Leading Seaman, Communications
Age: 22
Marital Status: single

David (Davy) is a Communications Technician, a lanky Scouser with a wicked sense of humour (when did you ever meet a Scouser who didn't?). He is responsible for SATCOM[7] aboard the ship so is either a hero or zero according to the availability of the Internet and phone services. He is somewhat stressed when we first meet.

"It's all just fucking shit, isn't it? I never wanted to join the Navy in the first place, I wanted to join the RAF as my old man had been in it and he'd had a lot of fun and done boxing and stuff but I just didn't do well enough at school. Anyway, this job is shit because I only have control of about 10% of the kit and when its's fine, it's fine but when the satellite is playing up, well, I get it in the neck big style."

What did he think of the mission? Was it worthwhile, was it worth risking his life for?

"Well, I don't know about that. I'm 22, what is worth risking your life for? It's not something I think about every day. At least there's the chance of a shag and I reckon we might get a run ashore in Port-au-Prince, at least that's what I've heard, what's your take on it?"

HMS REPUDIATE sights lands for the first time on Day 13, the low outline of the Turks and Caicos Islands off to our starboard as we navigate through the Antillas Mayores, to the north of Haiti and the Dominican Republic. As we handrail the northern coast of Hispaniola, we see coastal villages on fire throughout the archipelago and in the ghostly abandoned resorts and seaside developments. Davy's prospective run ashore, as yet, looks resigned to his locker.

Surname: Beaumont

---

[7] *Satellite Communications*

First Name: William (Billy)
Rank and Role: Warrant Officer Second Class (WO2), Royal Marines
Age: 32
Marital Status: recently divorced

William (Billy) Beaumont is a grizzled Scottish veteran of Iraq, Afghanistan and Syria, a leathery chunk of a man who could not possibly be anything else other than a career Royal Marine sent straight from central casting. He has piercing blue eyes which look as if they are constantly sizing you up for a wedding dress fitting[8], man or woman. It can be most disconcerting, but I have spent most of my career around men like Billy, and it bothers me naught. I interact with him for various reasons across the voyage, but interview him for the first time after his half-Commando first attempt to secure the port for HMS REPUDIATE to dock. I feel guilty for demanding his time. He is counting his casualties. At this point, we are anchored in Port-au-Prince Bay, protected from the storm brewing in the vast Caribbean lagoon, Gonave Island to our rear.

*"I mean, the boys had seen the Chewmans before, fuck-aye they had. When we down-selected for this job, the first question I asked was, how many of these cheeky wee fuckers have you killed, I mean really killed, liked a smashed head or a proper decapitation. You know, something to make sure they didn't fucking get up again. To get the company-plus here, I had to take some Crows[9], fuck-aye I did, but most of the lads had been blooded. London, Southampton, that fucking sorry business at Dover with the refugees."*

He stares at the floor, then looks up at me. You know the Thousand Yard Stare, the famous Don McCullin photograph of a US Marine at Hue, Vietnam, in 1968? Yeah, that.

*"It didn't make any difference. It didn't make any difference if they were aged 20 or 30, if they'd claimed to have killed 20 Chewmans or none. It was a rout. A total rout. We couldn't fight them. And if we*

---

[8] *Another daft joke. Royal Marines like to dress as women in order to reinforce their masculinity. Thus, it is not unusual for Marines to deploy to even the most hostile environments with extensive female wardrobes at the bottom of their bergen rucksacks. You know, just in case.*
[9] *A generic term for new or inexperienced soldiers*

can't fight them, if the Royal Marines can't fight them, then no one can fight them. Do you know what I mean?"

He looks at the floor again, and when he looks up, his eyes are full of tears. I want to give him a hug. I don't. But I did know what he meant.

"We had a plan. Rigid Raiders[10], dropped from the side of the ship, nice and low profile, flat hulls for getting in close and quiet engines, all the lads stripped down for fast action, no body armour or helmets, what was the point, we were not going to fight humans, so we just carried water and ammo. Clean fatigue, as we say. I took a hundred in with me, across fifteen little boats, all stealthy and quiet as fuck. We beached them about 5km north of the city, just beyond Pointe du Cul-de-Sac, left a small guard party of reluctant Marines with them, and started to yomp south-east, in three platoon groups, two up, one back.

"So our initial objective was to secure a suitable landing site for the Merlins and to recce for a possible temporary shore base from which the head sheds could start the search for Patient Zero. None of us really questioned at the time what a fucking mad mission this was, the place was in utter chaos, did they really think we could find one specific Chewman on this island, even if he hadn't already rotted away or been eaten by the others? But we did as we were told, and pushed inland along a south-easterly heading toward Toussant Louverture International Airport, about 7km from our landing beach.

"We encountered the first Haitian Chewmans in the suburbs of Port-au-Prince to the north-west of the airport. They were in advanced stages of decomposure (taken as evidence that the pandemic had started here), moved very slowly and posed little threat to us, our snipers armed with .50 Cals[11] taking their bloated heads off with ease at ranges up to and exceeding one klick. It became a bit of a game to the young marines and I had to remind them why we here and that those shadows of people they were happily popping like Figure 11 targets had been people once. And what was still going on back home."

I ask him what had occurred to make him think that this wasn't going to be the easy mission he had first envisaged.

---

[10] Small fast boats used by the Commandos
[11] .50in calibre, the largest possible round for a small arms weapon. The Marines have sniper rifles and Heavy Machine Guns chambered in this calibre.

"Well, it was when we started to approach the airport. We nearly always take the airports as quickly as we can - Basrah, Baghdad, Kabul - if you can secure an airhead then its the quickest way you can get mass on the ground and establish all the life support you need. Airports have got things which are really useful too, like hangars, maintenance facilities, power, hard buildings, perimeter fences, lighting - all good stuff for setting up a forward headquarters, not to mention the runway itself.

"So we sent a recce platoon in to Toussant Louverture. The perimeter fencing had been breached at many points, evidence of panic here as anyone with access to an aircraft had tried to get the fuck out of Dodge as things had turned to shit, you know, like Kabul in 2021. Abandoned light aircraft and the remains of a passenger jet which had collided with a pick-up truck cluttered the runway. The recce platoon sent up a small drone which gave them eyes in the sky, and also sent the video back to our TAK[12] devices in the main body. In this way, almost every marine had eyes on what happened next."

I ask him - what happened next?

"Our int was bad. We were not the only humans on Haiti. Why would we be? God, we were so arrogant, His Majesty's finest storming up the beach and strutting around a Caribbean island and partying like it was 1899 or something. So when the enclave of Haitians holed up in the Civil Aviation office - working on exactly the same tactical principles we were - saw us coming, they let the recce platoon enter the office compound across the long hot stretch of the airport parking apron, then hit every single one of them with shotguns fired from the windows of the building. And every single marine in the supporting force saw it happen, on their mobiles, tablets, laptops and on the big screens back on the ship.

"But what happened next......hmmm."

WO2 Beaumont pauses for breath and collects his thoughts. I have covered many wars and conflicts and I always feel guilt at this moment, when my journalistic desire requires a combatant, victim or - occasionally - a perpetrator, to relive an event they would much sooner forget. But that is my job.

"All the marines were wounded by shotgun blasts. A couple were dead or unconscious, but the rest had been pretty much incapacitated by

---

[12] Tactical Assault Kit, a software package viewable on phones, tablets and computers, showing mapping, video and positions of friendly forces, among other information

*wounds to the head, legs or upper body. I instantly regretted the decision to go clean fatigue. We watched in horror as a group of three Haitian men emerged from the office building, and one covered the others with a shotgun while they calmly disarmed the marines, kicking their rifles away from them and pulling them into a row, all facing one direction. Then a fourth man emerged from the building with a chainsaw and he-*

"He-"

"He.....walked slowly down the line of prone men and cut all their heads off."

I had heard this story, but it felt hard to believe and it was harder to hear it from a witness, even one viewing it on a mobile phone several kilometres away. WO2 Beaumont was an A1[13] source. I had no doubt of the veracity of his description, and it was verified by many other sources including the classified video source from the drone.

There are some which a war correspondent may witness which he or she will take to their grave.

This is such a thing.

Surname: Nelson
First Name: Horace
Rank and Role: Captain, Commanding Officer, HMS REPUDIATE
Age: 39
Marital Status: complicated, but mainly single(ish)

The intriguingly named Captain Horace Nelson, CO of HMS REPUDIATE, is a striking character. He resembles a young(ish) Michael Douglas circa Falling Down and has the melancholy air of man with the weight of the world on his shoulders, specifically commanding a warship and de facto the overall task force. In reality, he is man with a persistent link to PJHQ and cannot fart without permission. With great power, comes great political and media oversight. I am grateful for this meagre slice of his time - he is a busy, busy man.

I ask the Captain what his current plan was and how he intended to recover the remnants of his force.

---

[13] Sources of information are graded A1 to F6. The letter stands for the source reliability, the number for the information credibility. An A1 source would have a history of complete reliability, with information confirmed by independent sources, an E5 would be an historically unreliable source with a history of lying.

We are in his impressive wardroom onboard HMS REPUDIATE. He sighs, reaches for a bottle of Jura positioned strategically in his desk drawer, and pours us both a couple of fingers. It feels as if this is not the first time he has done this today (it is 1130 local time).

"Ah, yes, recovery. Very important to get the lads and lasses home, am I right? Yes, that is now my primary responsibility.

"So, after we lost the recce platoon, the remainder of the expeditionary force returned to the beach only to find the guard force slaughtered and turned by Chewmans. They took further casualties securing an extraction site for a Merlin to extract them, as their boats had been damaged.

"Once back aboard, we debriefed the survivors and re-assessed the mission, reporting back to PJHQ. They insisted we redouble our efforts, but as we were formulating a Plan B, we lost contact with HMS ALBATROSS, which was providing picket support in the Caribbean Sea."

What happened to HMS ALBATROSS?

"She.....she was sunk by a giant zombie fish. Or maybe a whale. Or a shark. We're not sure."

There is an awkward silence between us.

"It's an inexact science, to say the least.

"I can say, however, that whatever this creature was, it surfaced in Port-au-Prince Bay and made an attacking run on HMS CAPITA. It was only the intervention of a luxury yacht, flag unknown, which intervened and rammed the attacker, which saved our warship and all the souls aboard. I will never forget the sight of so many orange-overalled deck hands and bikini'ed ladies disappearing below the surface. Their sacrifice will never be forgotten."

In the end, the Marines were sent ashore for one last time and took significant losses from both locals and Chewmans while securing the airport. The surviving vessels were scuttled and just two RAF Atlas A400-M transport aircraft came in to collect the remnants of the task force. That could have been no more than 250 personnel, from a possible compliment of over 1300.

I am not allowed to say how many sailors, marines and airmen lost their lives in Haiti, but I counted them out.

And few of them came back.

# THE MAN WHO WOULD BE KING

Illustration by Mister Hughes

*34.26 degrees north, -118.33 east*

*The fortified enclave codenamed INDIAN, 10km northeast of Santa Barbara, CA.*

It would have appeared, to the casual observer, that the walls, defences and other obstacles originally intended to keep out the prying eyes, relentlessly flashing superlens cameras and yes, on one occasion, a *fucking de facto siege tower*, of the international paparazzi, were doing an equally grand job at keeping out the Chewman hordes, specifically the erstwhile inhabitants of Los Angeles. Admittedly, given the stylish location, this was one of the best dressed and most photogenic of undead hordes to ever attempt a mass attack on a protected location, but that was cold comfort to the inhabitants hunkered down within.

He watched the assault unfold safe behind thickly armoured glass, sipping at a decent malt which had been a present from his father's cellars back on one of the English estates. Or perhaps one of the Scottish ones. It could have been either, and it seemed a moot point now. Sadly, its supply was finite, and the opportunity for a replen seemed unlikely. He savoured its peaty, mossy taste, trying not to let the muffled bursts of fire from the security guards repelling the Chewmans trigger flashbacks. *Afghanistan, the Forward Operating Bases, raining down death from above.* Added to the effect was a reflection in the window from the large flat television on the opposite side of the room, inset into the view as if it were designed that way, SWEN YKS reporting live the chaos in Europe, cities burning and people dying.

His reminiscing was disturbed by a shrill ring from the housephone. The housephone? How many people had that number? Only a few. A specific few. *A very specific few.* He looked at the nine millimetres of dark malt in the bottom of the heavy glass, contemplated draining it, then decided against and placed it down on the oak occasional table under the phone. He took the receiver from the wall and placed it to his ear.

"Hello?"

"Hello. Confirm callsign INDIAN."

His stomach flipped. The codenames, first presented to him at age sixteen by his security detail. He hadn't heard them used since.....since *then*.

"Confirmed callsign INDIAN. Go ahead."

There was a pause at the other end, an audible clearing of throat.

"Menai Bridge is down. I say again, Menai Bridge is down. Confirm, callsign INDIAN."

He screwed his eyes up tight. *Dear Papa.*

"Confirmed, callsign INDIAN."

"*Danny Collins* and *Daphne Clark* are down. Confirm, callsign INDIAN."

Good god, his brother and his wife too. What the hell happened in Canada, they were supposed to be safe, protected by the Royal Navy and -

His discipline broke. "What about the children? Please tell me the children - "

"Callsign INDIAN, all subsidiary callsigns are down. I say again, all subsidiary callsigns are *down*. I am sorry......Your Majesty. Initiating protocol on other means."

The caller hung up. He stared at the mouthpiece of the phone for a long time, not believing what he had just heard. He picked up his whiskey glass and returned to the window. This time, he drained it, then threw the glass at the window with tremendous, frustrated force. There was an enormous bang but neither the whiskey glass nor the window broke.

She came running at the sound of the bang. She'd been bathing and was still damp, wrapped in a large and fluffy dressing gown, barefoot and wet hair spread across her shoulders. As she entered the room she glanced briefly at the chaos unfolding on the television but barely cast a thought to the battle raging outside their own windows. This was a standard, nightly occurrence, and time and circumstance had toughened her to such things. She placed her arms around his shoulders from behind and hugged him. She was used to the occasional outburst from him.

"Haz? What's the matter, honey? The war bothering you tonight?"

He closed his eyes and dropped his head to his chin. Tears did not come easily to him.

"They're gone, Meg. All of them. Papa, Willy, Kat.....the children. Oh, the children, Meg. They're all gone."

She pushed herself away from him then, gripped his shoulders and turned him from the window, lifted his chin and forced him to look at her. Her own eyes filled with tears immediately.

"What? No. No, that can't be. They were all safe, in Canada, with the Navy - that can't be. Haz, tell me it isn't true."

He shook his head, closing his eyes. When he opened them again, she was kneeling in front of him, her hands by her side.

"Your Majesty," she said, evenly and without a hint of inflection. Just stating a fact.

He pulled her to her feet roughly, angrily, and then stopped, taking his hands off her and holding them up, supplicant.

"I'm sorry, Meg. Don't say that to me. I can't-"

"You are. You just are. Deal with it right now. "

He backed away from her, shaking his head. He looked down into their compound again, the noise and firing from the towers and walls receding, the lights on the helipad illuminating the squat forms of an attack helicopter and a powerful twin-rotored transport helicopter, recent and now opportune purchases. He looked up at the reflected television images again. *London Bridge was burning down.*

"You know what you have to do now, Haz. You know, deep down. You always knew."

He turned to her, took a deep breath, and smiled. A single tear rolled down his cheek. That was all he had. A King had no time for tears now.

"Meggsy," he said. "Fire up the Apache."

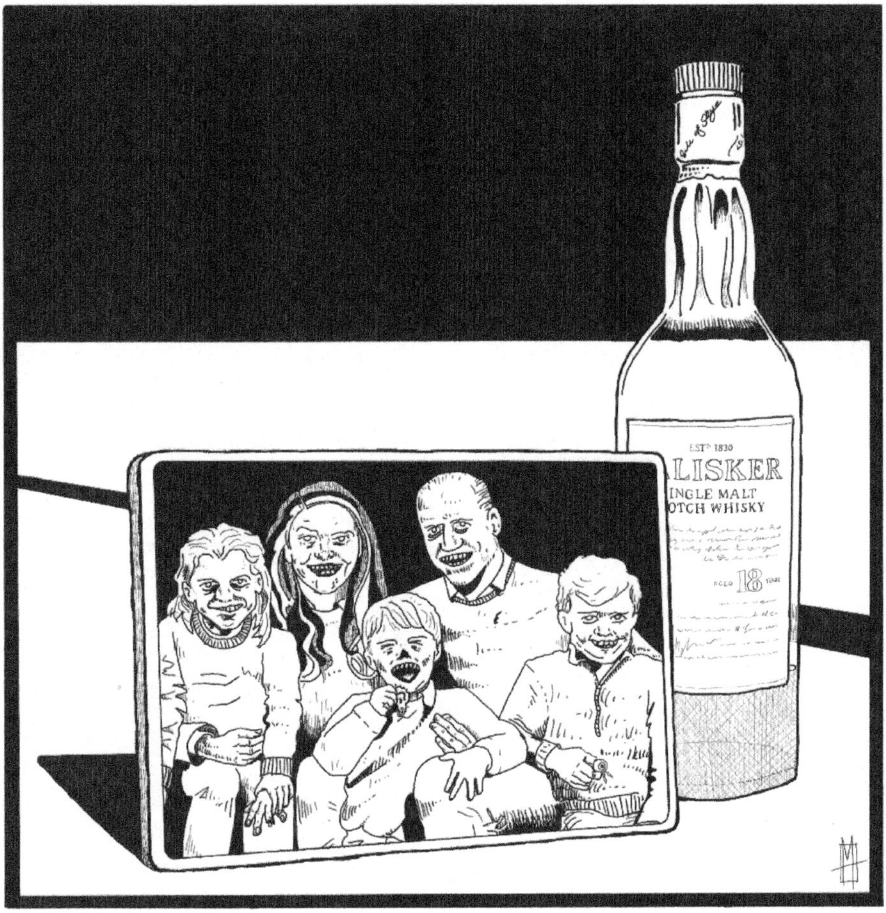
ALISKER
INGLE MALT
OTCH WHISKY
18

# THUNDER RUN

Illustration by Andrew Richmond

*The Hero is a staple of imaginative fiction. Without the Hero, dear reader, there can be no heroism, no heroics, no quest, no adventure, no derring-do and last-minute escapes from the jaws of death. Of course, we use the term 'hero' in its non-gendered sense, and include heroines in our definition. Think of the real-life heroes from history - Boudicca, Gandhi, Churchill - and the heroes from fiction - Indiana Jones, James Bond and Superman. We could talk about them all day. But we won't. Instead, we will focus on one very specific hero in our story. He is a hero the like of which you will have never seen before. Just an ordinary guy, about to do an extraordinary thing. His name, if you will, is Terry Mickle.*

*Before the Chewmans came, Terry was a hospital porter and part-time Amazon delivery and Uber taxi driver, just an ordinary Joe trying to make ends meet. He worked at one of the big hospitals in Birmingham, Britain's sprawling second city, the dead centre of the country (pun intended). He had never married, never had a relationship you could really class as a girlfriend (there was that librarian in 1995 but it is generally held that the other person needs to be aware of your existence before a 'relationship' can be declared - overdue book fines and being told to shut up do not generally count), and lived with his Mum until the ripe middle age of 55, when she died right before the start of the pandemic. So when the Chewmans came, Terry was scraping a living on the mean streets of Brum, and would have continued to do so, in a semblance of happiness, until......*

*Until. Some Heroes are born. Some are made. Others cast in the hot, sweaty, manly forge of battle. Terry sort of....tripped and tumbled into heroism. Dear reader, bear with us while we see just how such a hero is brought into existence, the wrong man, in the wrong place, at the absolute wrong time. Why don't we let Terry pick up the narrative? Luckily for us he has kept a diary since age 12 3/4 (precisely). We will speak again presently, dear reader.......*

**The Diary of Terry Mickle Aged 55 1/2**

10 January – Day 3700 (ish) of the Pandemic

Got up at 0600. Need a new alarm clock as this one sounds like punctured bagpipes. Need a wind-up one - we don't know how long the power is going to last. Squaddie shower, squaddie wash, couple of squats, up-down-one-three, the old military training never leaves you! Dressed and down for breakfast for 0615. Toast, margarine, marmite, coffee with three sugars to kickstart the day, no milk again so Coffee Mate it is, mate. And ready for action, again.

My old TA instructors used to say to me, Private Mickle, a good soldier always makes his bed, brushes his teeth, cleans his weapon. Well. I don't have a weapon (yet) but 2 out of 3 ain't bad. Or it might have been Meat Loaf who said that. It is easy to get confused these days.....

These days.......I do miss Mum. She used to make me a packed lunch every time I left the house. With the three jobs I sometimes had three packed lunches a day. Where did she get all the Tupperware from? I don't know.

*Dear reader.....Terry is nothing if not self-effacing. He knows exactly the dangers he is facing even on his mundane drive to work. Is he brave, because he was once almost in the Territorial Army? We think not. Terry was born great, he just doesn't know it yet. Things are about to get a whole lot hairier for Terry.......*

10 January continued........

My noble steed is the trusty Monkey. At least, that is what I call her. She's actually a Piaggio Ape, a three-wheeler electric delivery vehicle, a sort of a moped with ambition, attitude and glandular issues. It may be madness having a vehicle which requires electrical charging but to be honest, at the moment, electricity is ever so slightly more available than fuel, which is in negligible supply and prone to outbreaks of violence at the fuel stations. I admit that I don't really have the training to cope with that.

This morning, the Monkey is fully charged from a rare night of uninterrupted sparky juice. She is humming and ready to go. She's not mine - oh no, I may ride her like the Lone Ranger rides Silver but I don't own her, she is NHS Trust property and although I have the privilege of taking her home each night, she will be returned safe and sound when this current unpleasantness has come to an end. Which it must. Must it not?

My phone buzzes with a text. The cellular networks are collapsing like a naughty kid's Lego at the moment, so I am lucky to get some comms. My first job is at the QEH, Queen Elizabeth's (God Rest Her Soul) Hospital, over in Edgbaston. I am in Kings Heath, you know, the posh bit with gay folk and cats with tails and the ability to shut your window without trapping some bastard's fingers. That posh. You know what I mean?

**<PICKUP QEH. ONE LARGE PELICASE 1m X 0.5m, GENETICS LAB, ASAP. DELIVER TO MILITARY RESEARCH FACILITY 'X-RAY', EDGBASTON STADIUM>**

Roger that. A standard run, I have done this many times. The Genetics Lab to the Stadium is less than a mile, as the crow flies. But as the Monkey dawdles, along contested territory, then that is a Thunder Run, make no mistake.

**<PICKUP ACCEPTED>**

The Monkey awaits. I mount her gently, like a skittish foal, she has been known to fail me on occasion, but I am hoping not today. I push her start button gently, with respect, and her electric bugaloo purrs into life. As Sgt Horvath says in Saving Private Ryan (my all time favourite war film of all time), *"We're In Business."*

Alcester Road and Kings Heath High Street are spookily deserted. I should be used to this but I'm not. The bus stops around The Knob pub, once a de facto bus depot for Arriva and the numerous Number 50's into 'town', are now smashed and abandoned, much like The Knob and the Tesco Express. This was once one of the busiest bus routes in Europe. The frontage of the veterinary surgery gapes like an open wound, looted by people looking for drugs and medical supplies. Worming tablets and Cones of Shame will be of limited use, I feel. But I'm not an expert.

Similar story on the High Street. If Covid produced post-apocalyptic images of deserted travel agents, brochures peeling off shelves, then the Chewman Plague has Top Trump'd all that. Hollowed out buildings. Barricades and isolated islands of humanity, blokes in homemade body armour made out of carpet underlay, armed with brush cutters and kitchen knives, out foraging for provisions and useful stuff. *Been there, done that.* Roaming gangs of Chewmans, sometimes around twenty strong, shambling and flocking in what looks at first to be random patterns, but I am watching. Assessing. Nothing is random. And they are getting smarter and faster, in my humble opinion.

I cut hard along Moor Green Lane, skirting Highbury Park and the sadly unfinished railway station that would have connected us with 'town', now discarded like a child grows out of Lego. Swing a right at the roundabout outside the ostentatious Church of Scientology, now fortified like Camp Bastion, men in US Army uniforms patrolling its wired and Hesco'd [14] perimeter. I wonder what Tom Cruise and the rest of the Scientology mob make of this latest apocalypse? They seem to be going to a lot of effort not to die if they consider themselves immortal.

*Anyway.* Handrailing Cannon Hill Park and then a swing right toward the Stadium. I am about to enter a Tier One or Zombie Free Fire Zone, where martial law holds sway. The Stadium has been a developing military installation for several weeks, ISO containers and TDAs[15] crushing the delicate cricket creases. Saw a bit of pirate drone footage last time I pinched a bit of Internet access. Stadiums make great ad hoc military camps, in much the same way airports do. Landing space for helicopters. Power, water, lighting, perimeter, security. The road along the front of the stadium leading up to the A38 is a solid mass of barriers and includes two Challenger tanks and a Warrior armoured fighting vehicle.

This is where the nonsense stops.

---

[14] *HESCO BASTION are a brand of force protection product favoured by the NATO and Coalition militaries in the early 21$^{st}$ century. They are flat packed cages and hessian material which are easily constructed and filled with locally abundant material to make effective blast and security barriers. In Iraq and Afghanistan, that material was sand and gravel. In Birmingham, it was bricks from abandoned building projects. And sometimes a bit of Lego.*

[15] *Temporary Deployable Accommodation. Inflatable military tents used for accommodating troops, storage and hospital facilities*

**SWITCH OF HEADLIGHTS. STOP INSIDE THE PAINTED BOX. STAY IN YOUR VEHICLE. FAIL TO COMPLY AND YOU WILL BE SHOT.**

It's daylight so I don't have my headlights on. I stop the Monkey inside a box spray painted roughly on the road. I stay inside my vehicle. I don't want to be shot.

A soldier approaches me. He is kitted out in full battle rattle, body armour, the new full face helmet, assault rifle covered in bells and whistles. Seems overkill for Chewmans but what do I know? He stands two metres away from the Monkey and points his weapon at me. Grill on the helmet muffles and digitises his voice.

"*Identify yourself and your authorisation*," he says. He sounds bored. I fumble for a Ziploc folder in the Monkey and wave it in front of him. It contains a handwritten note from the director of the laboratory I courier for. He inclines his head, a vague move in the helmet, and asks "*Where are you headed?*"

"*QEH. I will be back here later with a package.*"

"*OK. There's heavy Chewman activity reported up there. Do you have a weapon?*"

I shrug. Not really.

He laughs. "*Then you're a dead man already. On your way.*"

He gives me a thumbs up. Is that it? My Ziploc could have contained a shopping list. Really? Standards are dropping by the day.

A barrier lifts, a tank roars into life and backs off a few metres, and I squeeze the Monkey through the little gap. As I 'speed' on (as best as the Monkey does), the gap is sealed behind me, and I head toward the A38.

As I cross the A38, I glance left and right. All I can see is the arse-end of Challies with their guns pointing north east and south west, the tanks sat a couple of hundred metres either side of the junction. So, whatever is going on at the Stadium is important. And I am a part of it.

The urban terrain closes in. Big Victorian piles repurposed into university and NHS buildings. Private hospitals, just as fucked over as everything else here. Chewmans shambling everywhere. The occasional military patrol, hard-targeting down the lanes, more scared of people than zombies. That's what I think, anyway.

*People scare me far, far more than the Chewmans.*

Turn on to Farquhar Road. Posh blue badge dogging site, some would say. Dangerous activity these days. I drive past double-parked abandoned cars – BMWs, Audis, a Bentley even – and enter the hospital complex proper by the statue of the nursing mother. The complex is *deathly* quiet. I turn down the hill and pull up in front of the laboratory. Double building, an old bit to the right and a new bit to the left. I'd been here many times, but today….today feels different….

I park the Monkey outside the car park barrier. As I approach the lab, I glance up at the multi-story car park next door, shocked at the wreckage of a Puma helicopter hanging from the edge of the roof helipad, gutted and burned. *Fuck*. What has happened here?

There is a litter of abandoned cars to the front of the lab entrance. This is actually a side entrance as the main entrance was through the hospital, and almost no one who worked there used that, under normal circumstances. This is far from normal circumstances. The security door, usually accessed by a proximity card, hangs from one hinge, like a decayed tooth. I enter, as gingerly as Ed Sheeran and Prince Harry eating ginger biscuits.

The lab has been ravaged. *Ravaged*. Debris and bodies litter the corridors and stairwells. I step over the bodies of people I knew, identifiable only by visible tattoos or unusual hair colours. I enter the bidirectional stairwell that always reminded me of a cinema, a theatre, or my uncle's house in London, bizarrely in the same configuration. The location I am after is to the left, on the second floor. I step over more bodies as I ascend the stairwell, and start to see evidence of what happened here. There are gunshot wounds and knife wounds, heads bludgeoned and people with limbs at odd angles, as if they have fallen – or been thrown – from the upper floors. This was *not* a Chewman attack. Sure, there are some munched faces here and there, the Chewmans have certainly been in here. But afterwards. After the Ravaging. This has been carried out by – I can hardly bring myself to call them this – *humans*.

I clamber over upended filing cabinets and storage units. Books, paper, glass and liquids everywhere. God knows what half of it is. I step cautiously, no doubt some of this is extremely toxic, and approach an inner glass office which has been carefully barricaded using mainly boxes of photocopier paper. There is a corpse splayed across the barricade, a lady, short grey hair, lab coat. She looks familiar. She has been shot three times in the back and her posture indicates she was trying to get inside the barricade. I wonder what is so important in there, and I also realise I have no real idea what I am here for, that without the scientists I have absolutely no chance of finding whatever it is I am here to collect. There are armoured pelicases everywhere. I will need to message the other laboratory if I am to figure out what to do. I pull out my phone and look at the screen – no bars, no signal. *Shit*. I will need to make my way to the roof, get some height and maybe I can scrape a bar.

But now, okay, let's see what this lady was so desperate to get to. Whatever it is, it may be of use to me. Or was she simply trying to get inside the barricade? Ride out the Ravagers attack? I start to hoik aside the boxes of paper, some of them shredded by gunfire, until I reach a glass door. The door and the surrounding windows are starred by bullet holes but have miraculously stayed intact despite the attack. I clear the door and step inside.

Small corner office, no more than 3m x 3m. It sort of reminds me of the office you'd expect J. Jonah Jameson to have in Spiderman, bursting out and shouting "Hold the front page!" or something. But this is not JJJ's office. There is a large desk, obscured by boxes which have been stacked high and then collapsed in a heap. I lift off one of the boxes. It is heavy, and the printing on the sides reveal that it contains ten times one litre bottles of antiseptic hand gel. Given that one litre of water at sea level weighs one kilogram (the TA taught me that), I am assuming that a litre of hand gel weighs perhaps a bit more. So each box at the very least weighs ten kilos.

The room smells. Flies buzz, awakened from sleepy shitty fly slumber by my presence. The room smells of cheap perfume, decay, and antiseptic. That's a powerful, throat-clenching combination. I carefully extract each box until I can see what is behind the desk.

I know her. I thought she was the boss of this lab but I think she was one of the deputies and the partner of another lady – ah! The lady outside is her partner. The actual boss. It all makes a sort of *perverted* sense now.

She's dead. *Of course she is.* Pinned and crushed and subsequently starved to death by the boxes of hand gel. She was a germophobe, in my subsequent research a rare but not unknown condition for a scientist. Someone obsessed with cleanliness to the point of an irrational phobia, driven by the current situation to desperate acts, hoarding supplies to the point at which the hoarding killed her, and despatched her partner under the proverbial bus. Not that we've seen a bus for a while. I take a moment, what we call in the Mob a 'Condor moment'. *Breath, Terry, breath.*

A phone rings. Not my mobile, not any mobile, but an honest-to-goodness bouncing handset phone trill. My hearing isn't great but it is somewhere in the outer office. I clamber over boxes and shit and get into the outer office. Desks are piled with debris and scatter but I locate the phone and pick it up.

"Hello?"

"Is that Terry? Terry Mickle?"

"Yes. Yes it is. Who is this?"

"That's not important. You need to listen carefully, Terry. Can you do that for me?"

Bloody hell, this was proper getting SAS Are You Nutty Enough?

"Yes, I can do that. I have training. I was-"

"Terry. You need to listen very carefully. Somewhere in that lab you are in is a bright yellow pelicase. Very bright, very yellow, very peli. Do you know what I mean, Terry?"

I did.

"I do."

"Good, Terry, good. I need you to find that pelicase Terry. Whatever you do, please do not open it. I say again Terry, please do not open it. Repeat that back to me, Terry."

Blimey.

"I will not open it."

"You are doing great Terry. Now, once you have located that pelicase Terry, I need you to bring it immediately to the Edgbaston Stadium, just like the original instruction. I am giving you the codeword GEORGINA, I say again, GEORGINA. This will get you through any military patrol or checkpoint. As for the Ravagers....well, you know the score, Terry."

"I do. I have training. I was in-"

"Good luck, Terry. God speed. Humanity relies on you."

Blimey.

Blimey O'Reilly.

*Humanity relies on me.*

I wonder if they knew that -

*Dear Reader, it is prudent of me at this point to reveal that our erstwhile hero had received very, very little military training at all. In fact, he completed no more than (at best estimate) fifty hours before his gout, asthma and general lack of what would be considered a useful backbone was discovered. This did not, however, stop Terry from dining out on it for the subsequent three decades, including a brief stint as an Army Cadet Instructor, to the point at which we may consider him what is known as a Walter Mitty, or, more colloquially, a 'Walt'. He was eventually publicly outed by a group of his own cadets.*

*However – let us not judge him too harshly. Every man, it is said, thinks less of himself if he has never served in the Army (particularly, I believe, if he has served in the RAF). And as I believe they say, cometh the hour, cometh the man. And Terry was, without a doubt, about to cometh………*

*Kerblimey.*
I wasn't trained for this. Did I mention I hadn't actually completed TA basic training? No, I probably didn't. I never made a big deal of that. *Feel a bit stupid now.* But it's far too late for that. Here we are, and here I am.

I've found the pelicase. It is highlighter pen yellow, it is hard to miss. I know I was told not to look inside but……

O.M.G!

You know that bit in Raiders of the Lost Ark when the Nazi goons look into the casket? It's a bit like that without the illumination and face melting. But otherwise – just like that. I would tell you but – I would have to kill you – and as previously outlined, I didn't quite reach that stage in my training.

None of this matters. I grabbed that big yellow box and I got the hell fuck out of there (pardon my French), the scheme is the thing, this is the mission, etcetra etcetera…..!

Damn. The Monkey won't start. I see a Chewman horde approaching from the road below the lab as I stuff the big yellow box into the back of the vehicle.

*Chewmans – Fahsands of 'em!*

They are not terribly fast but that doesn't matter when there are so many of them and my vehicle won't start. Push, push, and yes, thank fuck for that!

Impossible to wheel spin in the Monkey, so I give the middle finger out the window in lieu, good enough for government work. Let's go!

I retrace my route. Down past the statue of the nursing mother, hang a hard right. Past the car park and gym and pool, to the access road and another hard right. Train station, roundabout, retail parks, hard left at the big crossroads and the end of Bristol Road, heading back toward Edgbaston and the stadium. Good Lord, I am on the home run, I think, until I see stripped down jeeps and mopeds and other bits of my mobile junk vectoring in on me from left and right, and I realise I am crossing Ravager territory. A big, heavy, dirty, bin wagon swings across my path, spewing sewage.

The Ravagers. *Fuck.* Formed around the legendary Birmingham militant bin men, they had formed a post-pandemic militia equipped with heaviest and most formidable vehicles available in the civilian domain. I saw the big vehicle pass in front of me and then -

I don't remember a great deal after the explosion. I must have been hallucinating or something, because the first face I saw was that of the King. He was leaning over me, grinning, calling me a hero, shouting over the insanely loud beat of the rotors from his Chinook. He picked me up, threw me over his shoulder in a fireman's lift, and carried me on to his helicopter. He carried my yellow case easily in his other hand. I caught site of a huge red Maltese cross roughly painted on a white background on the fuselage. Crusaders!! As we passed under the hot downwash from the engines, I looked up into the face of an Angel, no, not an Angel, a Valkyrie, a dark-skinned beauty smeared with cam cream under a crewman's helmet, manning the machine gun on the ramp. And I knew then that I was in Valhalla, the eternal home of warriors slain in battle. The King placed me down on the deck with the other wounded soldiers, then resumed his place in the cockpit, and flew us the fucking bloody hell out of there.

*Dear reader, Terry's story, too good to be true? Certainly, our erstwhile hero was capable of hyperbole, of that there is no doubt, but there are many stories of the King and Queen flying medevac and close air support missions during this time, their helicopters emblazoned with a new symbol, one which came with some dubious historical cachet but which seemed to rally the people in the fight. And in the end, that is exactly what a flag is for. Is it not?*

*And as to Terry's fate? Alas, dear reader, that is where our story must end. Terry's wounds were grave, the military medical facilities sparse and rudimentary, and the doctors were callously - but justifiably - triaging and favouring the real soldiers who had been brought in. They didn't think Terry, in his 1985 DPM and pristine Silver Shadow trainers, was a real soldier.*

*But was Terry Mickle a real soldier? Well, dear reader, you know his story, so only you can decide.*

*Goodnight.*

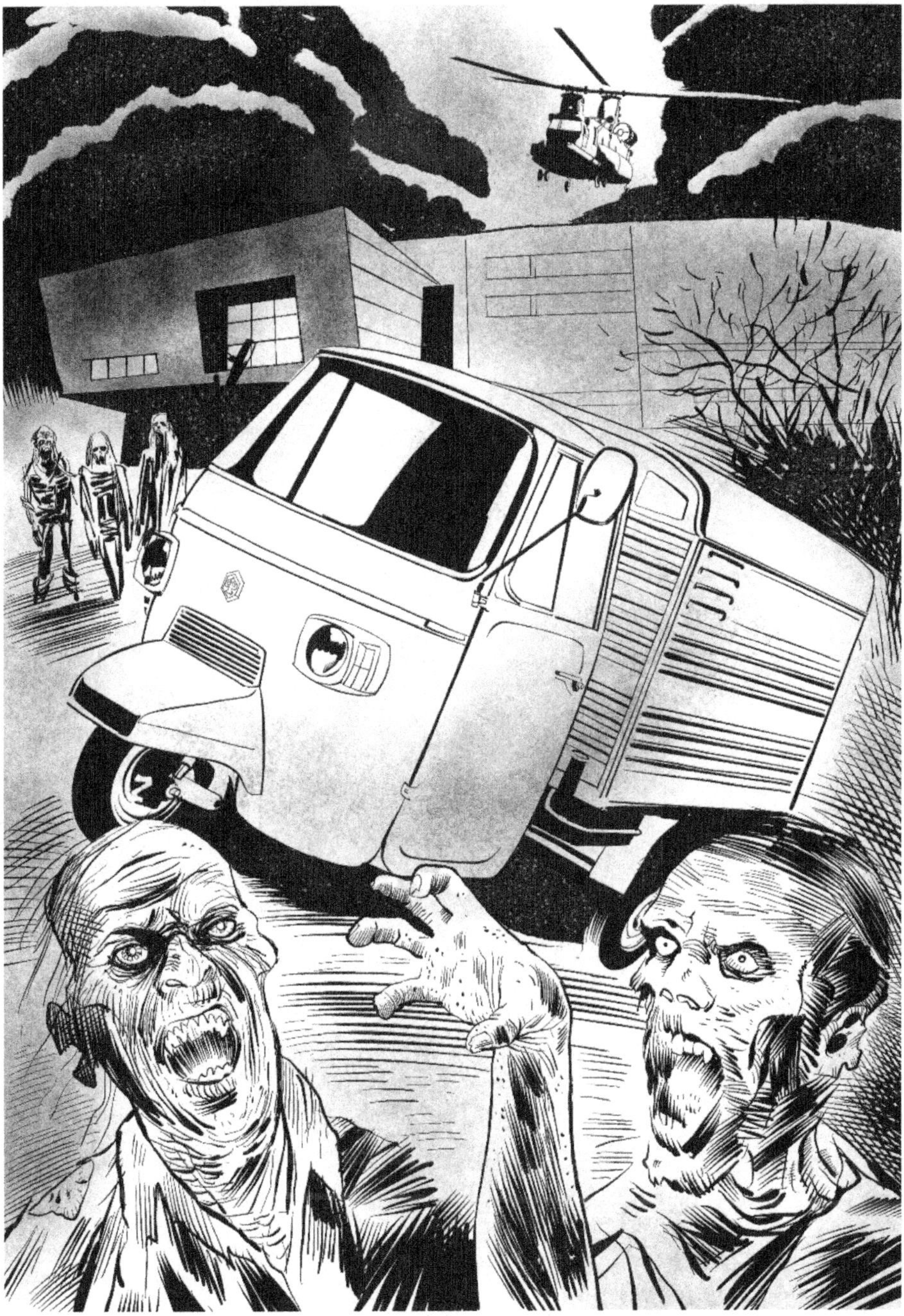

# ANOTHER BEAUTIFUL DAY AS A CORPSE

Illustration by Rik Rawling

*My name is George. Or Georgina. I'm not sure. Let's just call me Gee.*

*Life is difficult, and it's not surprising I can't properly remember my own name.*

*I'm different. The people around me aren't like me.*

*Well, in some ways they are. They shamble, and rot, and eat each other and normal people, and bits drop off them sometimes. I do all that too.*

*But I can think, and remember, and they don't do that, at least, I don't think they do.*

*I can love too. I had a husband once, Julian, a lovely man. And a son, Daniel. And a dog, Timmy. All gone now.*

*They thought Julian was the answer to this.*

*They were wrong.*

*It turned out, it was me.*

I remember. I remember what happened, when I was bit, when I turned. I was alone by then. They had taken Julian away, never to return. The soldiers, or sailors, or whatever they were, they just upped and left us to the Northern Lights Militia. And then Daniel had gone, just didn't return after I sent him to the village on an errand. I don't know what happened to him. I hope he was kidnapped by the NLM and that he's still alive. But he's probably not. He was still just a young boy, they shouldn't have taken him. But I hope they did.

Timmy pined away without Daniel. He lasted no more than three months, he just became more and more withdrawn and listless, until finally he wouldn't get out of his bed. I didn't have anything with which to put him out of his misery, I just had to watch him slowly die of a broken heart, and it broke mine. What adventures we had, Timmy, what adventures.

And then one day a traveller came into the village, had a drink in the NLM pub, started a fight and then turned, biting four or five people before someone fetched a shotgun and blew his head off. It was too late by then. I was in the market the day after, trying to barter for vegetables as usual, when the old lady on the stall sank her teeth into my arm as I reached for a bag of carrots. She barely scratched me, but I knew it was enough.

I'd seen enough people turn over the years to know what would happen next. The swearing, the lust for blood and meat, the loss of control. But even at the start I knew it was going to be different for me. For one, I had no one to talk to, so my swearing was confined to the odd outburst if I cut my hand chopping food or wood, it was hard to tell if that was out of the ordinary or not. Then, I had almost nothing in the way of a meat supply, so without coming into contact with other people, I had nothing to trigger me. It seemed as if I just died in my sleep one night, and then when I got up in the morning (I worked out later, it was in fact over several mornings) and started to wash my hands, my fingernails peeled off, right into the sink. I just stared at them, and knew that I had turned.

They came for us soon after that. I understand it became known as the Roundups. The nascent government started to assert itself and a new paramilitary force was established, based around the Navy but also incorporating some of the NLM and other militias, to get things back to the way they were.

It was never going to happen.

Humanity is dead. And no one cares.

But come for us they did. Late one winter's evening a small armada of Chinook helicopters flew over the village, the intense double beat of their rotors filling the valley, searchlights probing the hills. It was almost as if the noise and light was designed to bring out the Chewmans, of which I was now one. And it worked. Out we came.

Perhaps there was the smell of the meat too. Oh, but I shouldn't call it that, but yes, the smell of the meat and the blood and the sound of heartbeats and voices......a siren song, the flute of the Pied Piper, the Bisto Kids.....out we came, all the little huddles of Chewmen squirrelled away in their lonely hillside farms and woods, streaming down the valley, to where they waited.

It was a sight to behold. I would have been awestruck if I hadn't been one of the intended victims. There seemed to be hundreds of troops in full protective equipment – respirators, gloves, helmets – with long poles and hoops of braided steel wire hanging from the ends, like the sort of thing you might capture a tiger with. The Chinooks idled noisily on a flat piece of land, and I could see Chewmans from the village being captured by troops with the looping poles, directed roughly to the ground, then bound and dragged on to the waiting helicopters. The cargo bay of the Chinooks had been filled with huge steel cages and each Chewman was passed unceremoniously through a rotating gate on the rear ramp. Why were they doing this? They seemed content to shoot us before. Why were they going to such huge efforts to round us up? What possible benefit could we have to them, for them to keep us alive? Unless.....

I felt the heavy steel braid close around my throat and I was dragged to the ground. A soldier with a young voice screamed obscenities at me and kicked me while he still had me pinned. I felt nothing. Other soldiers bound my wrists and ankles with cable ties and then dragged me along the grass, throwing me through the rotating gate into the back of the helicopter. I was one of the last on board, and the cage was packed with rotting bodies. The ramp rose behind us, plunging us into darkness, and then the earth fell away and we felt the helicopter rise, gain height and then turn, taking us all to who knows where.

*Minutes. Hours. Days. Weeks. I have no idea. I am dead, what difference does time make? We are crushed inside the metal cage, bodies pummelled by the beat of the rotors and the vibration of the engines. There is no communication between my fellow Chewmans. Without any outside influence, I sense they are starting to consume each other, I feel wetness and changes in smell and hear. What if this journey lasts a long time? What will they find at the end, one huge bloated Chewman sat picking at bones in the centre of the cage, like Monty Python's Mr Creosote? That Chewman will not be me. But I feel the cage starting to shift, empty almost, as Chewman eats Chewman. Occasionally there is a flash of light through the helicopter's portal windows or forward doors, and the charnel scene is indescribable. Even dead, I am appalled. The images will never leave me, until the day I.....well, you know what I mean.*

Of course, the journey came to an end, but I cannot estimate how long it took. All I know is that the helicopter landed somewhere, at some point, and that the engines were switched off. The rotors slowly cycled down, and the deafening noise was replaced by men's voices and the snorting and hissing of the remaining Chewmans in the cage. The rear ramp was lowered and the interior of the Chinook was swept with light from powerful torches.

Perhaps half the Chewmans loaded in here remained intact and moving. The rest were dismembered, eviscerated, disembowelled, beheaded, torn asunder. I sat in a corner, chewing placidly on a thigh bone. The young troops vomited inside their respirators and refused to come aboard. Eventually an older contingent arrived, hardy men with just scarves tied across their faces, and they dragged the 'survivors' off the helicopter and across a narrow stretch of land.

It seemed that Darwin's survival of the fittest was not limited by death.

I am not sure how I knew we were close to the sea but despite having subdued sense other than smell, I could. This was a detention camp, one of the dreaded places set up during the first (now laughingly benign) pandemic and then repurposed once Britain positioned itself as a horrible place for a refugee to end up. There were high unclimbable fences topped with tight rolls of barbed wire. Huge imposing gates which looked like they could withstand a tank attack. Armed, angry faced men. And rows and rows of warehouses. Empty, concrete floored warehouses. No beds, no rooms, nothing. Just cattle sheds.

That first night. I cursed my sentience, called upon God to take me and spare me this, a dumb witness to the horror. But God wasn't listening. God had forsaken us all. Fuck you, God. And fuck Jesus and Mary and that fucking wee donkey too.

That first night. There was no attempt to control or segregate us. As we passed through the gates our cable ties were cut, giving us back the use of hands and feet. I couldn't understand this at first, and then as the night drew on, I understood. I knew what they were doing. They were trying to find me, the sentient one, the one they thought had been Julian, but what had happened? Had Julian expired under dissection and experimentation? Fallen to pieces under their knives? I would never find out. But I did work out that they were hunting for a sentient specimen, and they knew that whoever that was, would probably survive the night. And they would only then have a limited number of subjects on which to experiment, not the hundreds they herded on to the helicopters. It was all designed this way.

I knew I had to escape, that I didn't want to end up strapped to a table under the knife.

This was not the smartest bunch of humans. Elite troops are never left to guard prisoners, and the scale of this operation meant that half-arsed kids, NLM volunteers and semi-trained Royal Navy personnel formed the core of the guard force. They had yet to single me out, there were still too many other Chewmans to hide amongst, and it wasn't too hard to slip away from the melee inside the warehouse, hit the perimeter, and find a spot where a previous generation of internees had pulled up a section like badgers or foxes seeking the spoils of rubbish. I was out, and they hadn't even noticed they had lost their prize.

*Brighton.*

It was a long walk, well a very long stumble really. Despite my consciousness I was still Chewman, and decomposition is, well, a *bitch*. But something drove me on, heading west along the coast, along the A-roads and abandoned cars and trucks, not seeing another soul for days.
*(Do Chewmans even have souls, or has mine departed for more favourable climes?)*

*Brighton.*

I had spent many a happy week here, Before, with the Five, and we had enjoyed ice cream and the pier and Kiss Me Quick and candyfloss and arcades. I think it was that which kept me on my stumbling, shambling, feet-shredding pilgrimage. Also, I knew it would be my last. They would catch up with me. They would know that the only Chewman capable of escaping that camp was the exact one they needed. And I did not possess the faculties to hide, or hide my route or trail, in any way. So, I knew they would come, eventually.

The Grand Hotel. I remembered this as the place the Irish tried to kill a British Prime Minister. I didn't remember his name. But it got blown up at some point. They must have rebuilt it, because it was a beautiful building, even though the moss and dirt and bird shit covered it. I walked up its marble steps, through the delicate lattice work of the glassless conservatory along its frontage, and into its grand ballroom. There was a piano, a huge grand piano, covered in rubbish and dust but otherwise untouched. I sat down at the piano bench and lifted the fallboard, displacing a decade's dust. My hands fell naturally on to the keyboard, left and right.

Did Gee play the piano, Before? Before this? I flexed my fingers and let them drop on to the keys. Some of my fingertips were exposed bone and they slipped on the polished ivory, still clean and shiny after all these years. Something like a tune escaped from the innards of the piano. My hands moved with some long-buried muscle memory.

> *You must remember this*
> *A kiss is just a kiss*
> *A sigh is just a sigh*

Birds burst noisily from the balconies above me, startled by the sounds. I looked up but my hands continued to move, making noise, making……music?

> *The fundamental things apply*
> *As time goes by*

I stopped. That seemed to be as much Gee knew. Perhaps she had taken some piano lessons, Before. I looked down at my hands, but they lay dead on the keyboard, pressing down on the last chords. I tried to make them repeat, but they would not respond. Whatever had just happened, wasn't going to happen again. I carefully replaced the fallboard, stepped away from the piano bench, and walked out of the Grand Ballroom and the Grand Hotel.

*Brighton…….Blyghton…..Blyton? Was that Gee's name, Before? I shamble toward the sea, down the steps of the sea wall and on to the beach. Between the hotel and the skeletal remains of the Pier, a small warship lies beached on its side. It is as grey and dead as a washed-up whale. There are noises from within as I pass a few metres from its keel, it is home to creatures of some sort, Chewmans, humans, animal predators, whatever is within will not be friendly toward me. I make my way back up the beach and the promenade and on to the old Victorian pier.*
*Years of decay and decline turn everything into skeletons. Hotels, piers, humans, Chewmans. Everything gets stripped back to its framework, its basics, its structure. The Victorians built things to last*

*and the pier is a good example. Battered by the rain and the wind and the sea, she stands sentinel here, rusty and decaying but almost two hundred years old and still holding firm. I wander her abandoned arcades and bars and cafes and almost imagine the buzz and noise of people. The buzz……the hum….that…..? An engine?*

I had wandered to the end of the pier. Two very fast boats were approaching from the direction of the marina to my left. They were dark grey and were covered in tubes and wires which I assumed were guns and radio aerials. Dark clad men hunched in seats inside the open boats, and I saw them clearly as they made wide sweeping turns, churning spray and coming up alongside the pier for a better look at me. I looked down at their masked faces, all fear and urge to flight, now gone. One of them stood up in his boat holding up a short-barrelled weapon, and fired it at me. A strange projectile tumbled through the air toward me, trailing a thin tendril of smoke, and burst over my head. I felt something hit me and push me to the rotted wooden deck of the pier, applying a pressure all over my body. It was a fine steel mesh, and I was pinned down. A sudden electrical current passed through it, which made my limbs twitch and my eyes bulge, and I lost whatever vestige of awareness I had so far retained.

I regained what passed for consciousness sometime later. Days, weeks, I have no idea. The electric net had gone and I was bound and tied in the floor of a heavy, noisy, lumbering vehicle. I could see the boots of soldiers and their weapon muzzles resting on the metal deck. The deck was awash with mud, rainwater, oil, blood……*blood*……..! It made my nostrils flare and I emitted an involuntary grunt which earned me a kick to the side of the head.

"*Fucking watch it, Timmis, you cunt. Do you know how many stupid fuckers like you have died to get this cargo here? And here you are, kicking it about like a fucking football. Do that again, it will be the last thing you ever do with that foot, comprende?*"

"*Comprende, Sarge. I thought she was going to bite me.*"

"*She's an <u>IT</u>, and <u>IT</u> is tied up like a Christmas turkey, you stupid fucker. Now watch your six and stop fucking about.*"

They, or specifically Timmis, stopped fucking about. I felt the vehicle slow and the soldiers start to become agitated. The sergeant sent Timmis out to investigate. There was a brief period of silence and then some gunfire, shouting, sudden movement in the vehicle and then an almighty explosion and the vehicle turned violently through a hundred and eighty degrees. I flipped and bones smashed and flesh pulped, but that didn't matter to me. The soldiers were strewn around the vehicle, arms and legs and necks snapped. I was pressed in amongst them, limbs intertwined. Some were dead, some were immobile, and they screamed for their mothers as I started to feed.

Sometime later, satiated, I was dragged from the wreckage by more soldiers and there was much shouting and consternation at my discovery. Half of them wanted to tear me to shreds for what I had done to their comrades. The other half realised I am the cargo they were sent to recover. The intelligent half won, and I was bundled on to a military stretcher. Four soldiers ran with me up a road, and I could see a huge statue of a nursing mother, a bronze goddess now pock-marked with shrapnel and bullet holes. She gazed down at me, impassive, eternal, incorrigible, indestructible. She let me know I was in Birmingham, at the vast sprawling hospital complex.

The soldiers were fired upon as they hurried me around the perimeter road to our destination. I wondered what was going on here, why humans were fighting humans, and then I realised, it would *always* be this way. *Always*. Since the Before, everything was scarce. Nothing was created anymore. So, there were only things from the Before, and so they would fight over them. If they had enough things then they could hold out forever against the Chewmans. All they really had to fear was each other.

By the time I was carried into a building only two of the soldiers remained. I didn't know if the other two were shot or just got tired. They put me down in a lobby while they caught their breath and then a volley of shots, ricochets and sprayed plaster made them pick me up and rush me awkwardly up several flights of stairs, urged on by other soldiers and individuals in lab coats on landings, in doorways and stairwells. This was a laboratory, and it felt as if everyone has stopped work to see me arrive. And there was some urgency to my arrival.

We swept through a set of heavy rubber and plastic doors. There was a large table crowded with the apparatus of a lab, and one of the white coated scientists just swept it aside with his forearm, clearing it completely, glass and equipment crashing and scattering on to the floor. I was dumped unceremoniously on to the table and the soldiers exited, with a parting remark:

"You've got about fifteen minutes tops before we're overrun. Do you have an emergency protocol? I suggest you invoke it now."

I looked up into two masked faces staring down at me.

"Please.....don't...." I managed to croak.

They exchanged incredulous, horrified looks. Then a knife descended into the side of my throat, and I lost consciousness again.

*Darkness. Silence. So, this is it then? A Chewman death. No resurrection, no more shambling and rotting. Nothing. Nothing but peace. Where is my Julian? Gee is at peace.*

> *It's still the same old story*
> *A fight for love and glory*

*A sliver of light. A rush, to make me blink. I am in a small box. I look up into a man's face. Round, middle aged, bespectacled, utterly shocked.*

> *A case of do or die.*

"O. M. G." *he says.*

*And then there is only darkness again.*

*I miss you Julian. I will always love you.*

> *The world will always welcome lovers*
> *As time goes by*

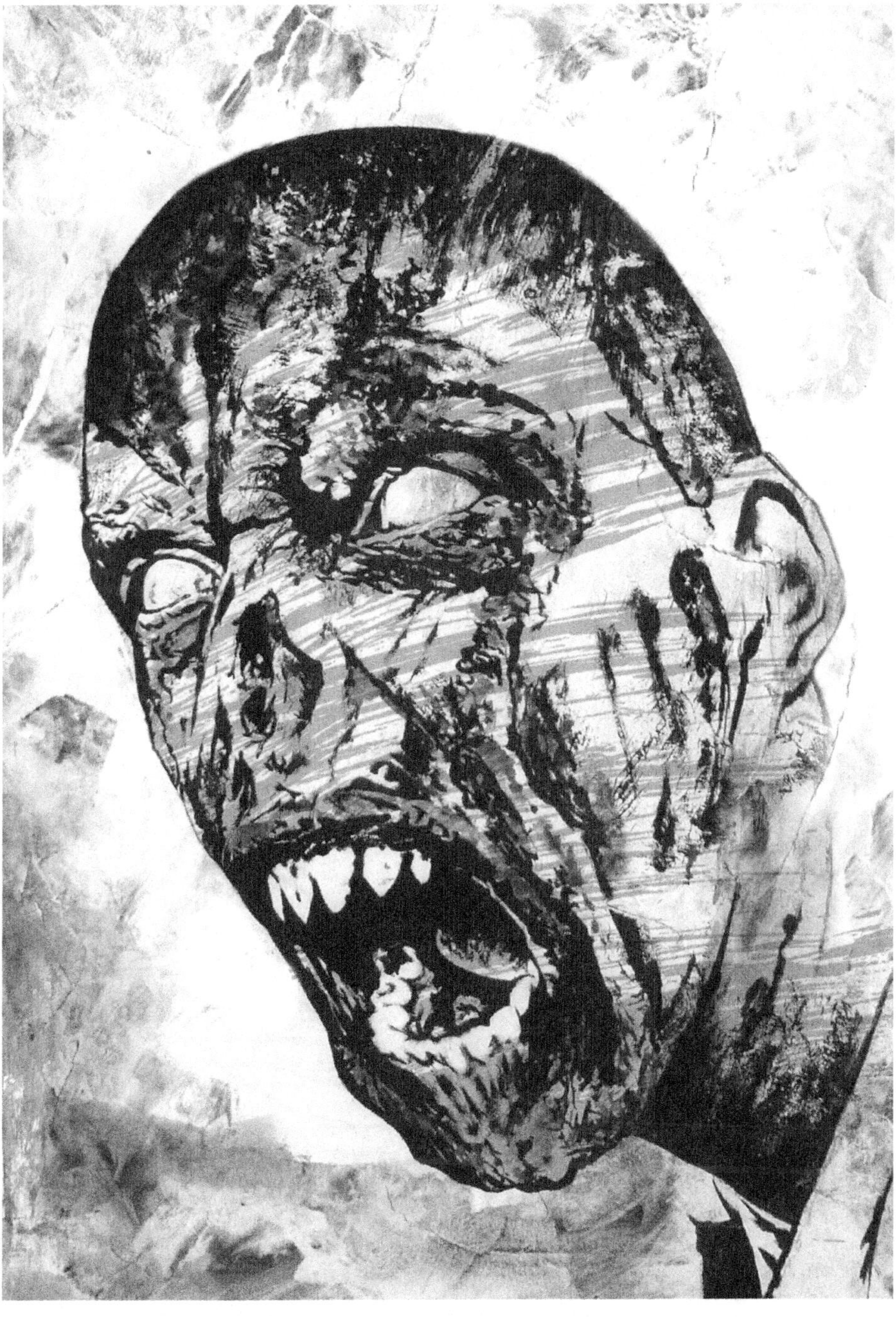

Illustration by Laurence Alison

*Don't Blame It On The Strangers*

*Don't Blame It On The Alt Right*

*Don't Blame It On The Vaccine*

Blame It On The Vegans


*The* **Virax** *may have been caused by the widespread popularity of Veganism in the early part of the 21st century, by genetic meddling in the food chain in order to create fully synthetic yet inanimate meat substitutes, and the resulting fungal side effects mutated into what we now refer to as the 'Chewmans', says* **Prof Alan Prophett, the University of What's Left of England.**


Much has been written over the years of the Virax and the 'Chewman Pandemic' which ensued. Certainly, the world is still reeling from this apocalyptic event, and it is difficult to estimate the global spread and infection rate, given the almost total collapse of international culture, media and communications (*except Mad Scientist of course!*). But we do have enough data, and information, and analysis in order to be able to lay the blame for this situation at one very specific door.

**The Vegans.**

We realise this may come as a surprise, and also may be interpreted as somewhat cruel. There are, probably, no more Vegans anymore. The reason for this, is that in a survival situation, dietary choices (as opposed to chemical imbalances or biological intolerances) will get you killed. When food sources dwindle, favour is with the resilient and the, well let's be frank, the less fussy. Darwin wasn't quite that specific, but that is what he meant.

But there is more.

Veganism interfered with the food chain. It was a strange dichotomy that as Vegetarianism morphed into militant Veganism, the desire to eat meat-like but meat-free products became predominant. This traditionally confused the omnivores and carnivores amongst us, as it was difficult to understand the mindset of wanting to eat bacon, sausages and mince, but not the naturally occurring kind we'd been happily consuming for millennia. The drive to create meat-like substitutes to satisfy the bloodless craving of the Vegan Horde led to rash decision making, cutthroat (metaphorically speaking) business practices, and wholesale disregard for the safety of the consumer. The Vegans wanted their sausage rolls, and everyone else could go fuck themselves.

You may recall some excitement during early government (remember that concept?) nightly briefings from Downing Street, and the alleged identification of Patient Zero from Haiti which led to the unfortunate misadventure history has dubbed Operation Voodoo Child. Of course, he was nothing of the sort and many British service personnel died confirming that point. Whenever a pandemic occurs, there is always a frantic race to find Patient Zero in order to see where the virus has come from, understand its roots, and get right down into its DNA in order to create the thing which will defeat it – the vaccine. Although the search for the vaccine continues to this day, our research has managed to positively isolate both Patient Zero and the source of the first infection.

You may be familiar with a low-priced chain of bakeries and sandwich shops known as Cleggs. Founded in the Northeast of England during World War 2, it had in the early part of the 21$^{st}$ century achieved a sort of faux-cool notoriety as a brand of choice – Northern, cheap, basic, with its own ironic clothing line. There entered into urban lexicon the concept of the Cleggs' Dummy – a large sausage roll handed to a screaming Northern toddler in order to shut them up.

*Let's cut to the chase* – Cleggs desire to become the predominant supplier to the hungry Vegans resulted in an unholy alliance with the Quorn company and created a mutant fungus which manifested itself in the Virax.

The Virax is therefore not a **VIRUS** – it's a **FUNGUS**.

Yes – humanity was put to the sword by a Vegan sausage roll and a noisy toddler in Crewe.

The story, we believe, goes something like this. Recent converts to Veganism Barry and Pauline were taking their son Darrall, 18 months old, on a constitutional through Crewe's quaint post-apocalyptic town centre, recently famous as the (undressed) set of a zombie TV series, oh the irony. Now, no one had bothered to tell Darrall that he was now Vegan too, and he was less than pleased with the limp, pink, unappetising thing he was handed in response to his noisy hunger pangs. But Darrall took the offending pastry and sucked and licked and gnawed and pawed at it in that disgusting way toddlers do, and in doing so, ingested the very first spores of the Virax.

We understand it took less than twenty minutes for the fungus to work its way through poor little Darrall's system. Try not to feel too sorry for him, he was a toddler from Crewe, he was hardly going to grow up and cure cancer. But when Mum reached forward to brush greasy pastry crumbs from his florid little face, he'd already Chewed, and took a sizeable chunk out of her forearm. As he wasn't yet verbal, it would appear he'd passed through the sweary bit.

So Darrall bit Pauline and Pauline bit Barry and Barry bit the lovely old man who ran the butty stall on the market. Then the lovely old man bit all the (specifically) early teenage girls who ran his stall, and they all went home early Saturday afternoon and bit all their brothers and boyfriends who were heading out to see Crewe Alexandra play Preston North End at 3pm that afternoon. So, there were lots of infected Chewmans in the Family Stand and the Singing Stand that afternoon and plenty of Preston NE fans got it in the neck later as Crewe Alexandra went down, inevitably, 0-3, including an extra time penalty.

With Crewe as Ground Zero the infection spread north, south, east and west with terrifying speed. Commuters took it to London where it grabbed instant hold in the densely packed capital. Shoppers took it to Liverpool One, the Trafford Centre and the Bullring. Air passengers took it to Paris, Berlin, Madrid, New York…..the pattern was set within days.

So here we sit now in the aftermath. This wasn't COVID-19, although that novel coronavirus killed almost 7 million people worldwide. The average death to infection rate was around 1-2%, depending on which country you were lucky enough to live in. The final death toll for the Virax is likely never to known as the institutions, infrastructure and intelligentsia whose role it was to produce these statistics are generally now long gone.

There is some hope. Although Ground Zero was long purged in a bioweapon strike, the focus has been on locating a Chewman exhibiting cognitive function and memory which might provide a clue as to the nature and 'future intent' of the Virax. After several abortive attempts, a candidate was selected and secured. As we are no longer required to abide by the requirements of the DPA and GDPR[16], I can reveal that the individual is Georgina Blyton, a mid-30s (at time of Chewing) female who was captured in Brighton recently. She shows significant signs of sentience and is an incredible opportunity to study the effect of the Virax on the human brain. At last update, she was being cared for by the XRAY Facility at Edgbaston Stadium, Birmingham.

She may be humanity's last, and greatest, hope.

**Prof Alan Prophett, the University of What's Left of England.**
*Want to fund my research? #gofundyourselfALAN*

---

[16] The Data Protection Act and General Data Protection Regulations

# The Recorders and Illuminators

## Noel K Hannan

*cut his professional teeth in the early 90s on comic books based on Night of the Living Dead, and here returns once again to his first love of zombies. I checked - loving zombies is NOT illegal, which is – phew – good news for all of us.*

## Andrw Sawyers

*Illustrator and coffee drinker – illustrates The Cell, Jubilee, To the Death, Aggros, Memoriam, H-Drive, Unit 666 and El Bunito having returned to the drawing board three years ago after a 25 year hiatus!!*

## Mister Hughes

*is a prodigiously Scottish and fiercely bearded musician. Active as an artist and writer in the UK underground/small press comix and zine scene in the '80s and '90s, he got back into illustration and design in recent years via poster and album cover design. Interests include writing about himself in the third person.*

## Andrew Richmond

*Writer, letterer, colourist, designer and publisher based in Bath, UK. He has appeared in Aces Weekly, The 77, Brawler, Reverend Cross, Sentinel, Future Quake, Zarjaz, Dogbreath, BLAZER!, Pandora, This Comic is Haunted, Gideon Gunn, Harker, Gravestown and Mad Girl. With much more to come!*
www.andrewrichmondart.com

## Rik Rawling

*a devout Yorkshireman and lapsed werewolf, Rik lives marooned in psychic exile in the mild mild West. Alternating between drawing, painting, design and writing, he heeds the Ballardian maxim of staying true to your obsessions.*

*Kick out the jams:* www.rikrawling.co.uk

## Laurence Alison

*is a forensic psychologist but in his spare time a comic writer (Hedrek, Warfighter, Out There) and occasional illustrator. Enjoying everything from Monster Fun to 2000AD and Warrior to Jimmy Corrigan, he has a wide interest and love of cartoons and comic books. His art tends towards the macabre and allegorical.*

## Jaroslaw Ejsymont

*born, raised, and educated in Poland. A professional graphic designer, Rzeszów University's Art Institute graduate, dedicated comic book reader, and occasional comic book artist and illustrator. He runs the Free Library of Comic Books in his hometown under the Academy of Comic Books in Rzeszów (RAK).*
www.behance.net/jaroslaw_ejsymont

## Marina Tsareva

*Ukrainian, born in Tashkent, Uzbekistan. I've started my career in the industry, working as a graphic designer of the print production. Recent years I work as a freelance illustrator, artist and graphic designer. I've won several international competitions in Poland. Several of the projects I've been working on were awarded in the UK. I work with worldwide famous bands, such as Cannibal Corpse on their brand coffee packages.*

# The After Credits Sequence...

Illustrations by Jaroslaw Ejsymont and Marina Tsareva

"Meg!"
"What is it, Harry?"
"Six o'clock, Meg. Farm on the hillside, what's going on?"

Meg leaned over the optical sights of the minigun hanging from the side of the Chinook. A farm sprawled across the low hillside below as Harry banked the Chinook so hard, she was looking directly down into it. A Chewman horde, a big one, was pouring up the hill at speed, overwhelming the fences and gates, overturning expensive vehicles and farm equipment in the courtyard. An old man, fat and slow, broke from a gate at the rear of the property and started toward out-buildings at the top of the hill, where a solitary Land Rover was parked.

"Come on, son, come on!" urged Harry, vectoring the helicopter toward the hilltop, thinking he might rescue this man.

Meg leaned closer over the optical sights. There was something familiar about this man, something she couldn't quite place. His stature, his gait.....anyway, the first Chewmans were snapping at his heels and he stumbled, two hundred metres short of his vehicle. Before the Chewman horde could wash over him, Meg put a short accurate burst into him and the vicinity.

"Meg! He was a slow old man, how could you do that?"
"It's quite easy, Harry. You don't have to lead them, as much."
"Shame, Meg, shame."

Harry looked at his instrument panel. Power, fuel levels, navigation. He glanced over at his co-pilot, Teddy. They had picked him up in Birmingham earlier and already this man was totally getting on his tits. Ex-SAS, survival expert, TV personality, former Chief Scout and devout Christian. His helicopter flying skills were rudimentary to say the least and since the Head of the Church of England had just rescued him, he had a beatific look on his face like Mother Theresa having just sucked off the Pope.

"Teddy," he said firmly, "Focus. Our business now is North."

*"You're in a blizzard, Harry!"*

Teddy had not endeared himself on the long flight north. The snow had started just north of Otterburn in Northumbria, familiar military territory, and thickened as they crossed the Scottish Borders. By the time they passed north of Edinburgh and started the long haul to the Highlands, Harry was flying purely on instruments, many of which were not receiving their usually reliable inputs, and ice and snow had started to build up on cockpit and fuselage.

Somewhere north of Perth a SARBE[17] alert on the Chinook's panels caught Harry's attention. Teddy leaned over.

"What is it, your Majesty?"

"Search and Rescue beacon, Teddy. A downed pilot, lost troops, hikers, I don't know for sure. But we should investigate. This far north, there hasn't been much Chewman activity."

Harry dropped the Chinook to within a few metres of the ground. The ensuing double blizzard from the storm and the rotor wash obscured his vision almost totally and he was completely reliant on instruments to let him know if he was about to make a very hard landing aka a 'crash'. Teddy whimpered in the seat next to him, completely out of his proto helicopter pilot comfort zone. Meg hung off the back ramp, trying to ascertain how far they were off the deck.

An intense blue light pulsed through the whiteout. Harry focussed on it and vectored in, guided by Meg's calm, measured observations. The ramp was down, and he was about to complete a risky manoeuvre he had never tried before, but that he had seen vastly more experienced pilots than himself execute in Afghanistan. His ramp gently touched the snow.

*One. Two. Three. Four. Five.*

"They're on!" yelled Meg on the intercom. "Go! Go!"

He pulled back on the throttle and gained altitude, up above the storm. The white dissipated and turned to black, he banked hard above the snow-laden clouds and regained his course. He was aware of a muscular presence at his shoulder.

"Fuck me.....I mean....your Highness....."

"It's actually your Majesty now, but let's not split hairs. Who are you and how many are you?"

"Your Majesty...crikey! I'm Wolfie and I am the team leader of an SAS patrol. There are five of us. When I say SAS patrol, we are all actually ex-servicemen and were scouting new locations for a reality TV show when-"

"I know exactly who you are Wolfie, and you don't need to explain anything to me. Settle your team down in the back and try not to scare any of the other soldiers. We have a motley bunch......but we are all we have....."

---

[17] Search and Rescue Beacon

Several hours later, the Chinook traversed the final hilltop and descended and into the heavily wooded valley of Balmoral. Harry held the Chinook at a hover several hundred metres away as Meg scanned the perimeter.

"There are some soldiers. Some heavy machine guns. I can't see anyone ready to fire on us. Bring us broadside, honey, show them the flag."

Harry turned the Chinook, showed them the Maltese flag roughly spray painted on the side.

"Barrels are drooping, Harry. We are good to go."

The Chinook cycled down noisily on the back lawn. Harry stepped from the cockpit, dumped his flight helmet, and reunited with Meg on the grass. They kissed passionately and started up the lawn to the house hand in hand. Harry was home.

"Your...your.....Majesty! I....I....wasn't expecting you!"

"Clearly, Prime Minister. But you are in my house."

The former Secretary of State for Levelling Up, the Cabinet Office, Housing and General Malevolence, now the de facto Prime Minister (given the unfortunate extended demise of the remainder of the Cabinet) was for once lost for words. He stuttered and stammered and spluttered, looking desperately to his deputy, the former Leader of the House of Commons and, usefully, the former first female former Defence Secretary. They were both acutely aware of the massive balloon glasses of brandy they held in front of them, first spoils of the foray into Balmoral's cellars. *Awkward.*

"Your Majesty," said the Prime Minister, puffing out his scrotum cheeks and executing what could only be interpreted to be a sarcastic half-bow, "may I ask what brings you to Balmoral?"

"I have come to dissolve Parliament," Harry said, drawing his Glock from its thigh holster and noisily racking the slide.

The Prime Minister's eyes went wide. "Your Majesty, that's impossible, I-"

And Harry shot him in the face. Right in his face. Two rounds, double-tap, bang-bang, the second hitting him before he even hit the ground. His brains spattered artfully over the lovely face of his Deputy.

She stood there shaking. Harry stepped forward and took the glass of brandy from her quavering hand, draining it in one shot.

"Prime Minister," he said. "I suspect I may expect your undying loyalty."

She dropped to her knees, squeaking in a tight pencil skirt, her eyes screwed tight.

*"Your loyal and observant servant forever, your Majesty. Forever."*

Meg felt a gentle tap at her shoulder. A small unassuming man was stood there, in old-fashioned and blood-stained camouflage, saluting. Next to him was a boy, similarly dressed, and standing smartly to attention.

"What is it, Terry?"

The man cleared his throat. "You should see this, your Majesty. The King too."

They followed Terry down a long, ostentatiously decorated corridor. The King placed his hand on the shoulder of the young boy.

"What's your name, soldier?"

"Blyton, your Majesty. Danny Blyton."

"And how old are you, Danny?"

"Eighteen, your Majesty."

The King barked a laugh. "This isn't the Army recruitment office, son. How old are you really? You can tell me, I'm your King."

"Thirteen, sir. But I can shoot, and I can fight."

The King gripped the boy's shoulder and guided him along in Terry's wake.

*That you can, son, and that you will, sadly. As will we all.*

Terry led them into an ornate anteroom where a huge flatscreen TV was situated. The rag tag troops from the Chinook and the Balmoral security detail were clustered around the TV. They parted to allow Harry and Meg a clear view of the screen.

On a Sky News rotation, the tickertape read RUSSIAN ZOMBIE INCURSION INTO POLAND. The visuals showed a loop of a bare-chested Russian president, visibly Chewed, riding a zombie bear at the head of a Russian Army of Chewmen and partially destroyed tanks, over the borders from Belarus and Kaliningrad into Poland. NATO, what was functionally left of it, had been mobilised.

Harry took a deep breath.

"Oh fuck," he said.

*Slava Ukraini!*

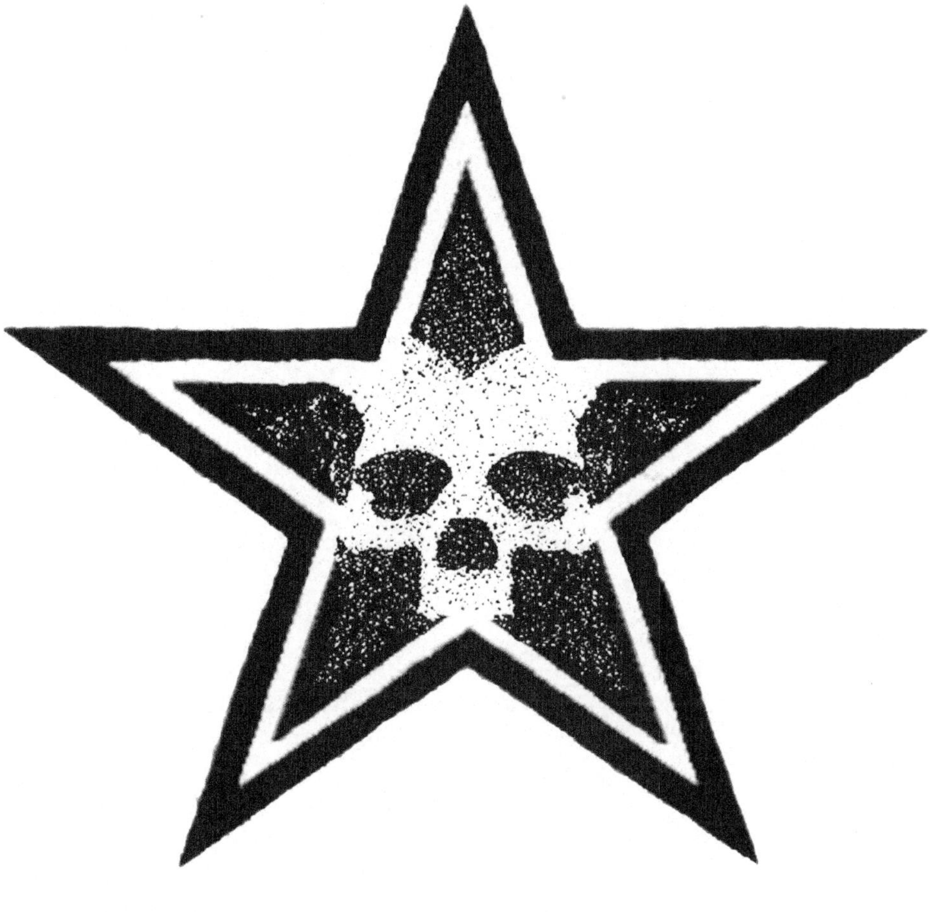

Printed in Great Britain
by Amazon